Y0-AFK-791

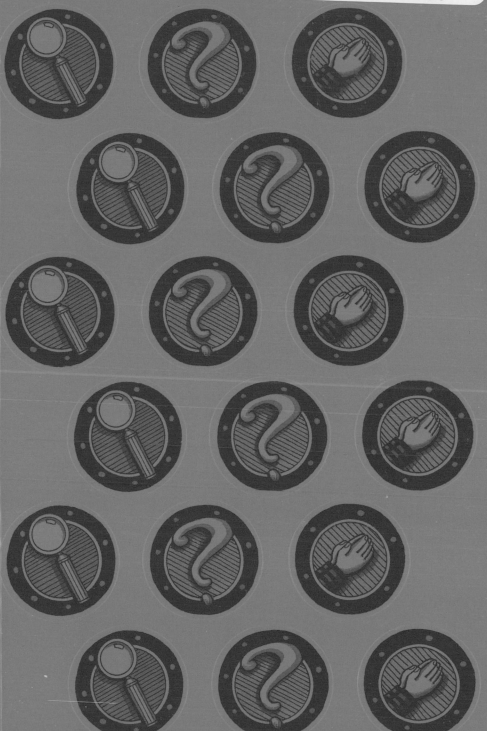

NEVER

TOO

SMALL

A Kids' Bible Study on Heroes

PAULA RINEHART

Gold 'n' Honey Books

Never Too Small

published by *Gold 'n' Honey Books*
a part of the Questar publishing family

© 1996 by Paula Rinehart
Illustrated by Tim Haggerty
Cover Designed by Kevin Keller

International Standard Book Number:
1-57673-008-5

Scripture quotations in the "Sticker Studies"
Bible study series for kids are from:
The Holy Bible,
New International Version (NIV)
© 1973, 1984 by International Bible Society,
used by permission of
Zondervan Publishing House;
New American Standard Bible (NASB),
© 1960, 1977 by the Lockman Foundation;
and The Living Bible (TLB),
© 1971 by Tyndale House Publishers

Printed in the United States of America

All Rights Reserved
No part of this publication may be
reproduced, stored in a retrieval system,
or transmitted, in any form or by any means
—electronic, mechanical, photocopying,
recording, or otherwise—without prior
written permission.

For information:
Questar Publishers, Inc.
Post Office Box 1720
Sisters, Oregon 97759

96 97 98 99 00 01 02 03 —

10 9 8 7 6 5 4 3 2 1

CONTENTS

WHEN PAULA RINEHART taught at Pantego Christian Academy in Arlington, Texas, one observation amazed her: as she read and discussed the Bible with her students, she found that they "taught" her almost as much as she taught them. Paula decided that someday she wanted to write a Bible study that would help boys and girls feel confident that they could read and understand the Bible for themselves.

Before she could do that, two exciting events happened: Paula and her husband, Stacy, had two children. Eventually, Allison and Brady became the ages of the children Paula had taught.

In addition to this series of Bible studies for kids, Paula has co-authored *Choices: Finding God's Way in Dating, Sex, Singleness, and Marriage* (NavPress, 1982, 1996) as well as a book on women and stress called *Perfect Every Time* (NavPress 1993). She lives with her husband and two teenagers in Raleigh, North Carolina, where she writes and works as a family counselor.

ACKNOWLEDGMENTS

MANY THANKS to the kids and the staff of Colorado Springs Christian School for their help in field-testing these Bible studies for kids — and to my own children, Allison and Brady, for permitting me to use some of the stories from their own experience here on these pages.

A NOTE TO PARENTS AND TEACHERS

THIS STUDY can be fun to do with your child or a group of children. And it's important that it be fun. Even if you do this study in a classroom, it should never feel like another class. Everyone's grown up on Sesame Street now! You probably remember someone saying this, and it's true: "It's a sin to bore a child with the Word of God."

This study is the perfect thing to combine with a date at McDonald's. Green, leafy trees in the park provide a great setting for this kind of talking.

When you discuss a scene in the Bible, talk as though both of you were there. You were watching from a nearby hill as young Joseph was led off to Egypt as a slave. You were in the tension-filled room with Daniel as he told his trainer that he would eat vegetables instead of the king's royal food. Your hands were helping to pull in empty nets on Peter's fishing boat after a long night with no catch to show for it. You were there.

Expect some exciting things to happen when you open the Bible with a child. He might just tell you what's really on his mind. And even more exciting — he might share something fresh from the passage that you or I had never noticed.

▼ Each Picture Sticker has a different picture on it.
In each chapter you will find a Picture Sticker question.
You'll be asked to find the sticker find the Picture Sticker
with the right picture to help answer that question.

▼ All of the Explore Stickers have a magnifying glass
on them. These stickers go with the questions called
"More to Explore." Each time you finish answering
one of them, place one of these stickers beside it.

▼ Each Message Sticker has different writing on it.
These stickers go with the questions called "Perfect
Fit," which give you important messages to remember.
You have to find the right Message Sticker to complete
the message.

▼ All of the SUPER Question Stickers have a big question
mark on them. After you've answered the study questions
in each chapter, put one of these stickers by your favorite
question.

▼ All of the Prayer Stickers have praying hands on them.
Use one of these stickers after finishing everything else
in each chapter. Stick one by something in each chapter
which you would most like to talk with God about.
Then take a moment to talk with God about this in
your own words. God will listen!

God Will Show You

I'VE BEEN LISTENING to Bible stories for more than thirty years now. But as I looked again at every one of the stories you'll study in this book, I learned something new — something that amazed me — from each one.

That's the way the Bible is: you can never get to the end of discovering something new. That's part of what comes from the Bible being a supernatural book.

When I first started reading the Bible myself, I would get turned around and rather lost. But as I kept reading, and truly understood that these were real people with a real God, I also understood that they were telling my story, too. I wanted to listen. I wanted to hear what God was saying more than I'd ever wanted anything. I hope that's what you want, too.

Because God *will* speak to any person who truly wants to listen to what He's saying. He speaks through the Holy Spirit and the Bible.

Each story in this book is one scene from the life of a hero in the Bible. In each of these stories, a person responded to God at an early age — just like you. That was a great part of the secret of the amazing lives they lived for God: they listened to Him before their ears got old.

Now is your chance. Even if you do this study with a parent or a teacher, this is *your* moment to listen to God. Now's your time to open the Book and see what God will show you.

CHAPTER 1

If God Gave Prizes

SANDY STOOD in the shadows of the church building. She was waiting for her older sister, Andrea, to pick her up after the midweek girls program at church. Tonight the prizes for the best Bible character costume had been awarded.

Finally Sandy spotted Andrea's car turning into the parking lot. She ran to meet it. As she opened the car door, her hot, angry words tumbled out.

"I worked for two weeks on my Queen Esther costume," Sandy said. "I was the only girl there tonight whose mother didn't make her costume. I designed my own, and it took me hours to make it. And I didn't get a prize! I didn't get anything!"

Andrea thought a minute. She remembered the last time *she* had been disappointed. "I know what you mean," she said. "It's always fun to win. But after all, Sandy, I honestly don't think God gives out prizes for how you look."

■　■　■

HOW *DOES* GOD choose a winner, anyway?

You're about to read a scene in the Bible that describes just that.

The nation of Israel needed a new king. God sent Samuel, His prophet, to a man named Jesse. God had chosen Jesse's son to be Israel's next king.

As they met together, Jesse had seven sons with him. Which one was the chosen king? How would God make that choice?

Open your Bible and read the story in 1 Samuel 16:1-13, then write out your answer to the following questions.

1　What instructions did God give to Samuel? What was he supposed to do? (Look at verses 1-3.)

2   Samuel saw Jesse's son Eliab first. Eliab must have been a sharp-looking guy, because Samuel thought for sure God had chosen him to be king. What did Samuel say to himself? (verse 6)

3   Who was missing from the lineup of Jesse's sons? And where was he? (See verse 11)
Write your answer here, then find the right Picture Sticker that goes with it.

4   The last part of verse 7 tells us something that God told Samuel: "The Lord does not look at the things man looks at. Man looks at the outward appearance, but the Lord looks at the heart." Think about what God says here. Then put those thoughts into your own words.

5   Each of us wants to be special — to be a winner. It's
    so easy to think only about what's on the outside. ("Is
    he tall enough to play basketball?" "Look how she
    French-braids her hair—she'll get the big part in the
    school play for sure.") As you watch television or listen
    to your friends, what do you hear that a person needs
    in order to be a "winner"?

MORE TO EXPLORE

6   Did you notice how carefully Jesse brought all of his
    sons before Samuel — all of them, that is, except one?
    Why do you think no one bothered at first to call David
    in from the field to be a part of what was going on?
    Add an Explore Sticker after you've answered the question.

7   (a.) Think about what's on the *inside* of you. Is there some attitude you want to ask God to change in your life? Is there an attitude you'd like to ask Him to give you more of? Take a few moments and write a sentence or two as a prayer that puts your thoughts and desires into words:

(b.) Think back to the scene that began this chapter. What would you say to Sandy that might make her feel better about not winning the prize she longed for?

8   Complete this sentence with the right Message Sticker:
What you *are* is more important...

Next put a Super Question sticker by your favorite question in
this chapter — the one whose answer means the most to you.

IN THE BACKGROUND of much of David's life, there stood a towering figure. Samuel was his name. He was one of God's first prophets. Like David, he was chosen by God when he was just a young boy.

In fact, Samuel was a gift through the prayers of his mother, Hannah. Hannah had no children. She promised God that if He gave her a son, she would dedicate him to the Lord all his life. (Could it be that someone prayed that for you, too, before you were born?)

Hannah took the young boy Samuel to live with the priest Eli, to learn how to serve God's people. Right away Samuel began doing something he would do all his life: *He spoke the words God gave him to speak, no matter what the consequences.* While still a young boy he told Eli that God would judge his family because of the sin of Eli's sons. This wasn't a happy message for Samuel to deliver — or for Eli to hear! But Samuel was faithful to speak the message God gave him.

Later, when Samuel was told to anoint David as king, the choice surprised nearly everyone.

The most unwelcome news Samuel had to deliver was telling Israel's King Saul that he had lost God's blessing. The Lord gave Saul a job to do, but he did only the part that appealed to him. Samuel delivered God's response: Because Saul rejected the word of the Lord, the Lord rejected Saul from being Israel's king. What painful words of truth!

But Samuel was faithful. And he urged God's people to stay faithful and to serve the Lord with their *whole heart.* Listen as his words of truth speak today:

> **Only fear the Lord and serve Him in truth**
> **with all your heart; for consider what**
> **great things he has done for you.**
> (1 SAMUEL 12:24)

THE ME I WANT TO BE:

WHOLEHEARTED

To be *wholehearted* is to jump into something with everything you've got!

Picture for a minute the dead of winter, when you're dying to have a day off from school. You wake up one morning and there are eight inches of snow outside. Then you hear the happiest words you can imagine: "No School Today." You wolf down breakfast, put on layers of warm clothes, and grab your sled out of the garage. You head for the nearest big hill.

While you're out there racing down the slope, you give it your all. Nothing else has your attention but the matter at hand — which happens to be sledding. Even as you huff and puff your way back up the hill, you are *wholehearted*. Nothing as minor as being tired or having to work hard will stop you.

God says that following Him is something like that: It's worth putting our *whole heart* into. It's worth giving everything we've got.

Put a Prayer Sticker by something in this chapter that you would most like to talk with God about. It could be something to thank Him for, or something to ask for His help on. Take a moment just to talk with Him about this, in your own words. God will listen!

CHAPTER 2

How God Out-Foxed
a Pharaoh

"HEY, JENNIFER, slow down!" Sarah called. "Let me catch up."

Jennifer stepped out of the flow of kids hurrying to catch the bus home after school. She waited as Sarah elbowed her way through the crowd to where she stood.

"Let's walk home together, okay?" Sarah asked. "I want to hear what you're bringing to Amber's slumber party Friday night."

Sarah was so excited about making plans that she didn't notice how quickly the smile fell from Jennifer's face.

Jennifer's answer took Sarah by surprise. "I'm not going to the slumber party," she said.

"Not going! What do you mean?"

She saw Jennifer bite her lip. Sarah kept talking. "Every girl I know is going. You always go to Amber's parties. What's wrong?"

Finally Jennifer spoke up. "My folks heard about some of the things that happened at her last party. They said I couldn't go to this one." Her voice trailed off to a whisper. "I guess I'll be the only who isn't there."

■　■　■

SOMETIMES "NO" is a hard word to hear. Moses had parents who were caught between a Pharaoh and a crocodile's jaw. Their "no" to Pharaoh saved Moses' life.

Moses was born during one of Israel's darkest periods. The Hebrews were slaves in the foreign land of Egypt. Pharaoh had men whose only job was to squeeze every last ounce of work and sweat out of these slaves. Even the children were made to dig ditches. Yet God blessed and multiplied the Hebrews in the land of their misery.

Pharaoh was worried that the Hebrews might rise up and overpower the Egyptians. He devised a simple but evil plan. Pharaoh commanded that every newborn Hebrew boy be thrown into the Nile River. He thought there would soon be no more strong, young Hebrew men to worry about.

God had a different plan — and it involved a special baby from a special family. Read their exciting story in Exodus 2:1-10.

1   The Hebrews were commanded to get rid of all their
     baby boys. So what did Moses' mother do (verse 2),
     and how do you think she might have done it?

2   The older Moses got, the stronger were his cries.
     Soon this baby boy would be discovered. But Moses'
     mother had a plan.
     (a.) What did she do? (verse 3)

     (b.) If you had been this baby's mother, what dangers
     in the Nile River might have made you afraid to put
     your baby there?
     *Write your answer, then find the right Picture Sticker
     that goes with it.*

3   Each woman or girl mentioned in this passage was
    used by God to protect the life of this boy who would
    grow up to deliver God's people out of Egypt. Who
    were these three special females?

4   The story of Moses' birth is full of unexpected twists
    and turns. Complete the following chart by writing
    down some of God's surprises for Pharaoh in the
    verses mentioned from Exodus 2.

PHARAOH'S PLANS AND EXPECTATIONS:	GOD'S SURPRISES:
Hebrew baby boys were to be thrown in the Nile.	(verse 5:) Moses was rescued from the Nile by Pharaoh's own daughter.
Because of Pharaoh's law, Moses' mother knew she might never see her baby boy again.	(verse 9:)
Pharaoh did not want the Hebrews to have any sons.	(verse 10:)

The boy Moses was brought to Pharaoh's house to live. There he developed into a strong leader. The Bible tells us, "Moses was educated in all the wisdom of the Egyptians and was powerful in speech and action" (Acts 7:22). If Moses had stayed in Pharaoh's house, he could have been a ruler in Egypt! The treasures of Egypt could have been his.

5   (a.) Read carefully Hebrews 11:24-26. What choices did Moses make later in life?

(b.) According to this passage, why did he gave up such a good life in Egypt and instead choose to suffer with God's people?

Moses became one of Israel's strongest and most godly leaders. He stood up to Pharaoh. He led more than two million Hebrews out of Egypt and through the wilderness to the borders of their Promised Land from God.

6   Moses had the experience of living in two homes —
first with his true Hebrew parents, then with the family of Pharaoh. What do you think Moses probably
gained from each experience? How did living in each
home help prepare him for the work God would
someday give him to do?
Add an Explore Sticker after you've answered the ques-
tion.

YOUR TURN

7   (a.) Have you ever thought that maybe God put you
into your particular family, with its strengths and
weaknesses, to prepare *you* for some important task in
the future? If so, what might it be?

(b.) Think back to the opening scene in this chapter. How could Jennifer get over the disappointment of being the only one whose parents said "no"? What advice would you give to Jennifer?

PERFECT FIT

8   Complete this sentence with the right Message Sticker: **You were born into your particular family...**

Next put a Super Question Sticker by your favorite question in this chapter — the one whose answer means the most to you.

CAN YOU IMAGINE taking your baby and setting him in a basket in a river? Moses' mother (whose name was Jochabed) did just that. Mothers through the ages have admired her faith and courage.

The Bible says that when Moses was born, Jochabed saw that he was "beautiful." Every mother, of course, thinks her baby is beautiful. But the infant Moses must have been especially handsome, which the Hebrews took as a sign of God's special favor on a child.

Jochabed was living under the most awful of evil edicts: Pharaoh had decreed that male children born to the Israelites were to be killed at birth. That was his way of keeping their numbers down. But Jochabed lived under a higher law, the law of God. So she hid her baby as long as she could.

If she continued to keep her child and the Egyptian authorities found out, they would come and kill her little boy. She had to come up with another plan. She must have really prayed, because her plan was so unique — so creative — that surely God must have given it to her.

Jochabed decided to appeal to another woman's heart. She must have known the spot in the Nile River where Pharaoh's daughter bathed each day. So she covered a basket with tar and pitch (to keep out the water) and set her baby inside. There at the river's edge, she hoped his cries would be heard and that the Egyptian princess would take pity on him.

Think for a minute what Jochabed risked to save Moses' life. There were the dangers of the river, first of all. And then suppose Pharaoh's daughter had said, "Oh, here's a Hebrew baby — but he's a boy. I'll turn him over to the palace guards to get rid of him." Jochabed might have never seen Moses alive again. As it was, Jochabed was allowed to continue to nurse him until he was weaned, but Moses became an adopted son of Pharaoh.

THE ME I WANT TO BE:
COURAGEOUS

IT'S EASY to have the courage to do something difficult or dangerous, if you aren't afraid. Usually when we think of someone who's courageous, we picture a person who stares without fear into the face of something that would make our knees knock!

But real courage is something more. Real courage admits the difficulty and the challenge and says, "But God…."

"It may be hard, *but God* will give me the strength."

"I may feel scared, *but God* will bring me through this."

At some point in your life, you're going to feel a little like Jochabed, wedged between a crocodile and cruel Pharaoh's command. In your own "impossible" situation, remember that courage is not about being unafraid. Courage is about trusting God to help you do what's right, even when you know you're afraid.

Put a Prayer Sticker by something in this chapter that you would most like to talk with God about. It could be something to thank Him for, or something to ask for His help on. Take a moment just to talk with Him about this, in your own words. God will listen!

CHAPTER 3

An Unusual Visitor

SIDNEY WISHED she wasn't the kind of person who noticed when other people felt shy or lonely or left out. But somehow she always seemed to know. Then she would find herself wondering what to do.

Try as she might, Sidney couldn't get Anne, the new girl in her class, off her mind. Anne hadn't made friends easily. But, as Sidney told herself, the reasons were obvious.

Anne's clothes looked like they'd been wadded up in a ball for weeks. Some days there was even an unpleasant odor that seemed to hang over her. But Anne's worst problem was that she stuttered. If you asked her a question, you knew you would have to wait a while for an answer.

For days now Sidney had watched Anne eating lunch by herself. In fact, Anne did almost everything alone. From a silent perch, she seemed to watch everyone else having fun.

Part of Sidney really wanted to befriend her. Whenever she prayed about Anne, her stomach would tighten into a knot. Sidney knew what she ought to do. Sometimes she could imagine herself walking up to Anne and just asking if she'd like to eat lunch with her and her friends.

But that was Sidney's problem: her friends. They would never understand. Worse yet, she could imagine their response: "Forget it! You go eat with Anne yourself."

Sidney was caught in a bind, and she didn't know how to get out.

■　■　■

HAVE YOU EVER known what you *ought* to do, and yet were afraid to do it because of what others might think or say?

Mary the mother of Jesus has been one of the most honored women in history. But sometimes we forget what a difficult spot Mary was in when she became the mother of Jesus.

Mary was engaged to be married to Joseph. In Mary's culture, engagement was almost the same as being married. If she were unfaithful to Joseph, he had every right to divorce her.

Remember as you read this story that Mary was only a young girl, a teenager about fourteen or fifteen years old. Put yourself in her shoes: How would you have explained to your family and your fiancé that an angel had visited you and told you of an unbelievable event?

Read Luke 1:26-38, and think about what Mary faced and how she must have felt.

1   The Jews felt that God blessed those who were rich and powerful. Yet the angel Gabriel came to a young, poor girl who lived in a small town called Nazareth, to tell about a special privilege God had for her. How did Mary respond at first? (verse 29)

2   The angel assured Mary that she didn't need to be afraid. She would become the mother of God's Son. What were some of the other things the angel told Mary about this Child she would carry? (verses 31-33) *Write your answer, then find the right Picture Sticker that goes with it.*

3   Mary then asked Gabriel a simple question: How could she have a child, since she had no husband? (a.) How did the angel answer her? (verse 35)

(b.) Gabriel then mentioned someone else. Elizabeth, Mary's relative, was an older woman who had never been able to have a child. Now she was pregnant. Look at verses 36-37. How do you think this news might have encouraged Mary?

4   Look at Mary's last words to the angel in verse 38. What did Mary mean by this? How would you put it in your own words?

5   Mary must have been in the habit of saying "yes" to God. What does Mary's attitude tell you about her commitment to the Lord?

6   (a.) Look at Proverbs 3:5-6. How might the memory of these familiar Scripture verses have encouraged Mary? *Add an Explore Sticker after you've answered the question.*

   (b.) How do these verses encourage you?

YOUR TURN

7   (a.) Is there anything you feel God wants you to do, but you haven't done it because you're afraid of what someone else would think? If so, after praying about it, write out a short plan of what you think God wants you to do, and how you will do it.

(b.) In the scene that opened this chapter, Sidney is in a difficult situation with Anne. What are her options?

(c.) What do you think she should do?

P E R F E C T   F I T

8   Complete this sentence with the right Message Sticker:
     Even when you do the right thing…

IN MARY AND JOSEPH'S TIME, being engaged was much like being married. If a person wanted to break their engagement, they would have to write out a "bill of divorce." Being engaged to be married was no small thing.

Imagine Joseph's surprise when the woman to whom he was engaged told him that she was pregnant, but that the Holy Spirit was the baby's Father.

Jewish law said that if a woman was "unfaithful" to her husband or her husband-to-be, then the man was justified in divorcing her. Joseph was a good man, the Bible says, so he considered breaking off the relationship quietly, in a way that would not embarrass Mary publicly.

Then God intervened. In a dream He told Joseph not to be afraid to take Mary as his wife. The child she carried was very special. Conceived by the Holy Spirit, this child would grow up to be the Savior. God told Joseph to name this baby Jesus.

Joseph listened to God, and he willingly obeyed. His willingness brought him the honor of guiding this special Child through His boyhood and His growth into manhood. What a privilege!

As we admire the willing obedience of both Mary and Joseph, and desire to be more like them, we can pray this prayer:

> **…sustain me with a willing spirit.**
> (PSALM 51:12)

WE'RE TAUGHT to look for heroes. People with lots of talent who make a big splash at whatever they do — these are the folks who win the awards. They get interviewed on television. They have trophies on their bookshelves. They get put in the front of the class.

It's not that way with God. God is the One who possesses all true power and wisdom. In His temple, the Bible says, everyone cries "Glory!" So God has no reason to be impressed with earthly all-stars.

Instead, He is looking for a person who is *willing*. Being willing means that even though you don't have all the answers, and even though you may not be able to do a perfect job, and even though your friends may think you're crazy, you are still ready to do whatever God asks of you.

As God makes His path plain to you, then like Joseph you're willing to follow Him. Even if the path is strange, you go ahead and take it, because you know that *God* knows where it's all going to lead.

Put a Prayer Sticker by something in this chapter that you would most like to talk with God about. It could be something to thank Him for, or something to ask for His help on. Take a moment just to talk with Him about this, in your own words. God will listen!

CHAPTER 4

Actually,
I'd Prefer Spinach

TYLER PUSHED OPEN the door of the convenience store and
walked in, grateful to be out of the hot summer sun. One
quick glance around told him what he needed to know. Eric,
Bud, and Jason were huddled in the back corner, totally
absorbed in video games.

Tyler hurried over to join them.

Eric looked up from "Black Tiger" just long enough to give Tyler his something's-up grin.

"Hey, what's happening?" Tyler asked. It was obvious that Eric must have something on his mind besides their usual late afternoon combination of skateboards and video games.

Eric pointed to a silver-colored box sticking out of the back pocket of his jeans. Cigarettes.

"Here we go again," Tyler thought. Whatever Eric suggested, Tyler knew that all the other guys would go along. All summer long Eric had been full of crazy suggestions.

"Where did you get those?" Tyler asked.

"I'm not telling," Eric replied. "But I'll give each of you guys one as soon as we get out of here. Just let me finish this game."

Tyler was glad for the delay. He needed time to decide what to do. "But I'm *not* wasting my lungs on those skinny little rolls of tobacco leaves," he told himself.

■   ■   ■

WHAT DO YOU DO when the choice before you seems easy to everyone but you? How do you muster up the nerve to say, "Thanks, but no thanks. Not me. I'll pass"?

That's exactly the situation Daniel faced in the Bible. He was one of about fifty young Jewish men — actually boys between the ages of thirteen and seventeen — who had been carted off to Babylon to serve King Nebuchadnezzar.

Just as God had warned, His people were taken as captives and slaves to serve their enemies in the foreign land of Babylon.

But God had not forgotten them. Daniel was God's man for this special moment in history. His obedience to the one true God placed him in the most important spot in Babylon.

Read Daniel 1:3-21 to study what happened.

1   Nebuchadnezzar and his officials tried hard to change
    these good Jewish boys into Babylonian men. Look
    at the king's three-year plan for accomplishing this.
    (a.) What were these men to be taught? (verse 4)

    (b.) What were they to be fed, what else was done to
    them? (verses 5-7)

    .

2   The king's "choice" food had been offered as a sacrifice
    to idols before it was served as dinner. What did
    Daniel decide in his mind, and what did he do about
    it? (verses 8 and 11-13)

3   Nebuchadnezzar was a man with a bad temper.
     Because of this, what could have happened to
     Daniel's commander — and to Daniel? (verse 10)
     *Write your answer, then find the right Picture Sticker
     that goes with it.*

4   Think carefully about Daniel's situation. What reasons
     or excuses for going ahead and eating this royal food
     could a person have come up with?

5   Daniel was sure that after ten days of vegetables and water, God would prove him and his friends more healthy than those who had eaten food sacrificed to idols. How did God honor their faith in Him? (verses 15, 17, and 20)

6   Verse 21 says that Daniel served in the king's court in Babylon until the year of King Cyrus. That means he served God there for nearly seventy years! Read Daniel 2:48 and describe what happened to Daniel as he served God faithfully in a foreign land.

7   Come up with some words that describe Daniel.
This crossword puzzle will help you. *Add an Explore
Sticker after you've answered the question.*

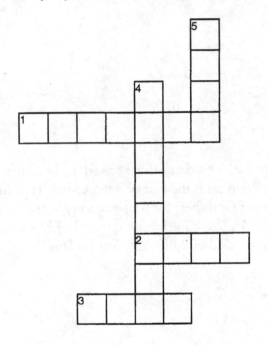

ACROSS:
   (1)   If you aren't afraid, you have _____.
   (2)   Not soft or weak.
   (3)   Having a lot of nerve; rhymes with gold.
DOWN:
   (4)   Full of faith.
   (5)   Someone who makes good choices is _____.
(Answers at the end of this chapter.)

8   (a.) Think of a likely situation in your life in which you would be tempted to compromise — to give in when you know you shouldn't. What would tempt you?

(b.) If you remembered Daniel's example in your own time of temptation, how could it encourage you *not* to give in?

(c.) Think again about Tyler's situation in the scene that opened this chapter. What could Tyler do now? What can he say that will free him from taking the first step down the road to a bad habit?

9   Complete this sentence with the right Message Sticker:
     By saying "no" to a few things now, you can...

*Next put a Super Question Sticker by your favorite question in
this chapter — the one whose answer means the most to you.*

IN THE SPOTLIGHT:

NEBUCHADNEZZAR

HAVE YOU EVER KNOWN somebody with a "big head"? Everything has to be his way. Only his ideas count. He has to be the star of the show.

That's a fair description of Nebuchadnezzar, the king responsible for carting off Daniel and his friends to Babylon. King Nebuchadnezzar had about the biggest head of his day. He let everybody know that he was king of Babylon the Great, a city he claimed to have built himself.

But no matter how big and important Nebuchadnezzar thought he was, there was something troubling his life that he couldn't control: his wild dreams! His latest one had him terrified. In it he saw a giant tree that was suddenly cut down by a command from the sky, and stripped of all its branches, leaves, and fruit. Then the stump that was left seemed to be a person, but the person's mind was changed from that of a man to that of a wild animal.

The king was sure there was a message in all this. But none of his magicians and other Babylonian advisers could explain it.

So the king sent for Daniel, who had already proven himself as a man God used to reveal His mysteries. After hearing about this dream, Daniel had bad news for the king: The tree was Nebuchadnezzar himself. He would be struck down with insanity, and would live like a wild animal. Therefore Daniel urged the king to humble himself before God and to confess his sins, but Nebuchadnezzar didn't take the advice.

A year later, the dream came true. Just as he was boasting about Babylon's greatness, he lost his mind. He was driven away from his people, and for seven years he lived like a beast and ate grass. Nebuchadnezzar's pride got the best of him.

His sanity returned to him only after he recognized the truth: he was just a man, and worship belongs to God alone.

HUMILITY WAS WHAT Nebuchadnezzar needed to learn.

Humility is about a person's willingness to recognize how much you depend on God. You don't go around acting big, because you know you're like everyone else. You know you need God. Humility lets you get close to God and close to other people.

Sometimes we get humility confused with weakness. But those two are really opposites of one another. If you're humble, you're strong enough to admit you don't have all you need in yourself. It's the people who are proud who are truly the weakest, and in the most danger.

Put a Prayer Sticker by something in this chapter that you would most like to talk with God about. It could be something to thank Him for, or something to ask for His help on. Take a moment just to talk with Him about this, in your own words. God will listen!

Crossword answers:
1-across: courage. 2-across: firm. 3-across: bold. 4-down: faithful. 5-down: wise.

CHAPTER 5

From a Pit to a Palace

MATT SHOVED OPEN the door to his brother's room without even bothering to knock. Lee looked up, startled, then tried to act cool.

"What's your problem?" Lee asked.

"Why is the front wheel bent on my new dirt bike?" Matt almost spit out the words as he continued. "I told you never to ride that bike without asking me! I can't help it if you wrecked yours. You know I waited months to get this bike, and—"

"I had to run an errand for Mom," Lee interrupted. "It was raining, and I slipped on Mr. Garrett's driveway and bumped into his garage door."

Matt stood for a minute and glared at his brother. Lee could always find some reason, some excuse to cover up for his mistakes.

"I don't care how you did it," he snapped at Lee. "I just want my dirt bike back the way it was before."

Matt's head was hurting. He felt his eyes brimming with tears. He stepped back. He wanted out of there quick.

■   ■   ■

CAN YOU REMEMBER a time when you felt you were treated unfairly, when you got the short end of the stick, as they say? Who hasn't had an experience like that!

In all the Bible, no one (except Jesus Christ) was treated more unfairly than Joseph — a guy whose brothers sold him into slavery.

Our look at Joseph begins when he was seventeen, in that teenage twilight zone — not a boy, but not quite a man. We'll read about two parts of Joseph's life. In the first part you'll see some of the reasons why Joseph's brothers turned against him. But watch closely... the Joseph you'll meet in the second part has changed.

As you read, ask yourself this question: What kept Joseph from becoming a bitter, angry man who wanted nothing but revenge?

Start by reading Genesis 37:2-8, as you meet Joseph the teenager.

1   How did Joseph's brothers feel about him? (verse 4)

2   List the reasons you can find for why Joseph's brothers felt this way (verses 2, 3, and 7 each contain a hint). Remember that Joseph's colorful coat marked him as his father's favorite, the one who would receive a special inheritance.

Joseph's brothers plotted to kill him but decided to sell him into slavery instead. Then, just as his life in Egypt seemed to be getting better, he was falsely accused and sent to prison. There Joseph did a great favor for another prisoner. But when that prisoner was released, he forgot Joseph and did nothing to help him get out of prison.

3   Joseph sat in a prison cell for two more years. He
     must have often thought back over his life and the
     grief his brothers had caused him. How might Joseph
     have been tempted to feel toward his brothers and
     toward God?

Joseph was finally released from prison. God blessed him with
such wisdom and skill that Pharaoh made him second in
command over all Egypt.

    Joseph had spent thirteen years as a servant and prisoner
in Egypt, but he *learned* through those tough times. This is
what he learned: God was in control of all that had happened
to him. God blessed him *in spite of* the pit and the prison and
the unfair punishment.

    After seven years of abundant food, there was a great
famine in that part of the world. Joseph's brothers traveled to
Egypt to buy food. They spoke with Joseph many times, but
they did not realize the man before them was the brother they
sold into slavery twenty-two years before!

    Then Joseph decided it was time to tell his brothers who
he really was.

4   Read Genesis 45:1-8, one of the most emotional
     scenes in the Old Testament. From this passage, how
     do you know that Joseph was upset? (verse 2)
     *Write your answer, then find the right Picture Sticker
     that goes with it.*

5   Joseph reminded his brothers that they had sold him
into slavery. He hadn't forgotten what they'd done. But
had Joseph *forgiven* his brothers? How do you know?

6   Three times in this passage, Joseph told his brothers
that *God* had been at work in his life. God had allowed
bad things to happen to him in order to bring about a
bigger and better purpose.
     Find and write out the short phrases where Joseph
tells what God was doing (in verses 5, 7, and 8).

MORE TO EXPLORE

7   Think back over the whole story. Joseph's dreams
had come true. He was a great ruler; his brothers
bowed down to him. But Joseph *himself* had changed
a lot from the boy who wore his special coat and told
his grand dreams. Describe Joseph *before* and *after* he
went into slavery and prison?

(c.) Do your best to unscramble these words that
describe Joseph — before and after.
Add an Explore Sticker after you've answered the question.

Joseph Before:	Joseph After:
DRPOU	VGIINFROG
TTTLEAETAL	TRISUNGT
SSYOB	ESWI

8   (a.) Think of a time in your life when you felt as if you got a bad deal. Or maybe there was something you had looked forward to, but it was a giant disappointment; you knew it shouldn't have turned out that way.

    Take a minute to think about this. Then turn your thoughts into a prayer. Ask God to show you how He wants to use that bad deal for *good* in your life.

(b.) Think back to the scene that opened this chapter. Is there any hope that Matt could forgive his brother? How can Matt deal with his situation?

9 Complete this sentence with the right Message Sticker:
   God is able to turn the worst that can happen...

*Next put a Super Question Sticker by your favorite question in
this chapter — the one whose answer means the most to you.*

JOSEPH HAD eleven brothers (they're all named in Exodus 1: 2-4). The oldest of these brothers — and the one who seemed to care the most for Joseph — was named Reuben.

Apparently Reuben had serious guilt pangs about selling Joseph into slavery. Like the other brothers, he must have been more than a little jealous of Joseph, who was clearly his father's favorite. But Reuben was horrified that his brothers would think of taking Joseph's life. In fact, the Bible says that Reuben talked them out of killing Joseph. "Throw him into this pit instead," Reuben suggested. He intended to come back and rescue Joseph. When Reuben discovered that the other brothers had sold Joseph as a slave to some traders passing by, he tore his clothes in grief and regret.

Reuben must have always felt bad for how things had turned out for Joseph. Much later, when things were also going badly for the brothers in Egypt, they believed that all these troubles must be happening to them because of how they had treated Joseph years before. Then Reuben spoke up: "Didn't I tell you not to sin against the boy? But you wouldn't listen! Now we must give an accounting for his blood."

Reuben was also very protective toward their youngest brother, Benjamin. He promised his father, Jacob, that he wouldn't let any harm come to Benjamin (unlike what had happened to Joseph).

From all that we can tell, Reuben realized how wrong it had been to sell Joseph into slavery, and always wanted to make up for what he'd done.

> He who covers his sin will not prosper;
> but whoever confesses and forsakes them
> will have mercy.
> (PROVERBS 28:13)

THE ME I WANT TO BE:

FORGIVING

WHEN SOMEONE does something that irritates you only a little, it's usually not hard to forgive him. You get over it quickly. But what if someone hurts you in a way that really costs you something important? Then it's much harder to forgive.

Joseph was faced with the challenge to forgive some people very close to him (his brothers) who did something that should have totally wrecked his future. Sure, God did miraculous things in Joseph's life in the foreign land where he was sent as a slave. But Joseph could have easily nursed his anger toward his brothers for the rest of his days.

How do we know that Joseph instead was able to forgive his brothers? He seemed genuinely glad when he finally saw them again so many years later. And he was willing to provide the food they needed for themselves and their families.

Another clue about Joseph's forgiveness is found in the names he chose for his sons. Joseph named his first son Manasseh, a word meaning "forget." God had helped Joseph forget the trouble caused by his brothers. His second son was Ephraim, meaning "twice fruitful." God had blessed Joseph in the land of his affliction. Yes, Joseph had chosen to put his past behind him and focus on the God who gave him prosperity.

Forgiveness — real forgiveness — can be hard work. But it lets us go forward without dragging the past behind us. Forgiveness lets us enjoy God's blessing on our lives.

Put a Prayer Sticker by something in this chapter that you would most like to talk with God about. It could be something to thank Him for, or something to ask for His help on. Take a moment just to talk with Him about this, in your own words. God will listen!

Answers to chart: BEFORE—proud, tattletale, bossy. AFTER—forgiving, trusting, wise

CHAPTER 6

A Small Spark— a Big Fire

THE GAME looked over. No team could overcome a four-touchdown lead with three minutes left to play. Rick's dad reached over and turned off the TV. "Let's go down to Dairy Queen and grab some milk shakes. Sound good to you?"

Rick's eyes lit up. It wasn't every day that he got both a chocolate milk shake and time alone with Dad.

Dairy Queen wasn't crowded that day. Rick and his dad were able to get a corner booth. While they drank their shakes, Rick's dad propped his feet on the other bench. He was obviously in no hurry.

"How have things been going at school these days?" he asked.

"You mean, how's it going with my friends?" Rick corrected.

His dad smiled, and nodded.

"Well," Rick answered, "it's okay I guess. Jeff's parents are getting a divorce. He never talks about it, but I can tell it bothers him. Honestly, Dad, he smarts off about everything. Sometimes I'd like to let him have it."

"Why don't you invite him to go with you to that Christian concert coming up next weekend?" his dad asked. "Maybe this is just the point in his life when the Lord can get his attention."

"Oh, Dad," Rick answered, "you know how my friends at school are. They're okay guys, but nobody ever mentions Jesus or the Bible or church or anything like that. I'm the only Christian I know. And what can I do?"

■　■　■

DO YOU EVER feel your life is only about as special as a single chocolate chip in a pan of fudge? Keep reading. We're going to study a fascinating story of how a proud, important man's life turned the corner toward God because of one little suggestion made by a young servant girl.

It was during a particularly low time in Israel. Bands of Arameans regularly invaded Israel's territory and took captives to serve as slaves. Israel seemed powerless to stop them.

Read this story in 2 Kings 5:1-17. Let your mind replay the scenes like a movie projector. You'll move from the house of a mighty Aramean army captain named Naaman to the front door steps of Elisha the prophet of God. And you'll end up in the waters of the Jordan River.

But don't move too quickly! Notice a certain character — a little girl — who comes on the stage to say only one line.

1   There are many clues given in 2 Kings 5:1 about this man Naaman. List as many as you can find. Who was he? What was he like? What was his problem?

Leprosy was the most dreaded of diseases. It could cause the loss of fingers, hands, feet, or arms. Naaman could not have stayed a valiant warrior very long unless his leprosy was cured.

2   (a.) An unnamed girl had been taken captive from Israel to serve Naaman's wife (verse 2). What bold step did she take? (verse 3)

(b.) This girl had been stolen from her family and put to work as a slave. What attitude *might* this girl have had toward Naaman's problem?

Any hope for Naaman's cure seemed to be found in Israel. Word was sent to Israel's King Joram who was frightened. What could *he* do for leprosy? Nothing. And Naaman, the man who needed the cure, was the commander of the enemy army. King Joram had every right to be afraid.

3   Now Elisha the prophet of God enters the scene. Elisha told the king to send Naaman to him. Naaman went to the prophet's house with a big parade of horses and chariots (verse 9). He might be a leper, but he was a powerful leper.

(a.) What did Elisha do next? (verse 10)

(b.) What was Naaman's response? (verses 11-12)

4   (a.) What argument finally made Naaman willing to follow Elisha's strange instructions? (verse 13)
After selecting your answer, find the right Picture Sticker to go with it.

(b.) After Naaman followed his instructions, how was he changed? (verses 14-15)

5   Later Naaman asked if he could haul some of Israel's dirt back to his homeland (verse 17). This was his way of saying he would serve their God. Think back now through the whole story. Who was the small spark that started the big fire?

6   Read 2 Corinthians 12:9-10. What encouragement can this verse give us when we think we aren't smart enough or old enough or good enough for God to use us?

MORE TO EXPLORE

7   Naaman's story tells that "his flesh was restored and became clean like that of a young boy" (2 Kings 5:14). What changes do you think took place on the *inside* ? *Add an Explore Sticker after you've answered the question.*

8　(a.) Right now, ask God for the opportunity to take a small but bold step for Him (just as the servant girl did). Ask Him to show you how He can take a little thing and turn it into something much bigger than you'd imagined.

(b.) In the scene at the beginning of this chapter, do you think Rick is right about his influence on his friends? Is he so outnumbered that he ought to just give up? What do you think he should do?

PERFECT FIT

9　Complete this sentence with the right Message Sticker: **When God blows on a small spark...**

THIS STORY of Naaman's servant girl is actually a chapter from the larger story of Elisha, God's bold prophet to Israel. Elisha was taught by Elijah. Then, when Elijah died, Elisha took his place. Some of the most amazing Old Testament stories come out of Elisha's life.

Do you remember the woman whose small son died, and a prophet came and lay down on top of the child until the boy's flesh became warm and he came back to life? That was Elisha! Or have you heard the story about the pot of stew that was poisonous until Elisha threw in a handful of flour to make it eatable?

Perhaps one of Elisha's best moments came when bands of Syrians were attacking the Israelites. They had surrounded the city where Elisha was staying. Elisha's servant was with him, and was nearly in panic. But Elisha prayed and asked God to open the eyes of the servant. Then the servant saw that God's horses and chariots were all around, ready to fight for them. They were not outnumbered after all!

From the moment God first called Elisha, he obeyed and never looked back. He killed the oxen he was using to plow his field and had a big farewell feast for his friends. That was his way of saying he was leaving his home and his farming to answer God's call on his life.

Elisha spent more than fifty years demonstrating the reality and power of God to His people, Israel.

> Know that the Lord Himself is God;
> It is He who has made us, and not we ourselves;
> We are His people and the sheep of His pasture.
> (PSALM 100:2)

THE ME I WANT TO BE:

FAITHFUL

HAVE YOU THOUGHT ABOUT the challenges this young servant girl was up against? Can you imagine being taken to a foreign country to serve the people who were responsible for your capture and who probably killed the rest of your family? What a hard situation to have a good attitude in!

This servant girl shows us what it means to be faithful to God in spite of terribly difficult circumstances. In her mind, she was serving God — and she did that by serving the people around her. She took advantage of an opportunity to show that the Lord of Israel was truly God. He alone could cure something as impossible as leprosy. Because she was faithful to share this truth at the right time, her master came to know the living God. And we read one of the most exciting stories of the Old Testament.

Can you think of a time when *faithfulness* has marked your life, when you did what was right and true, in spite of everything?

Put a Prayer Sticker by something in this chapter that you would most like to talk with God about. It could be something to thank Him for, or something to ask for His help on. Take a moment just to talk with Him about this, in your own words. God will listen!

Say "YES" To MorE ThiNgS LateR.

Into The BEST.

THaN HoW YoU LooK.

It BECoMES a BRight FlamE.

For a SpECial REaSoN.

Not EVERYoNE UNdERStaNds.